The Carp in the Bathtub

BARBARA COHEN

Illustrated by

JOAN HALPERN

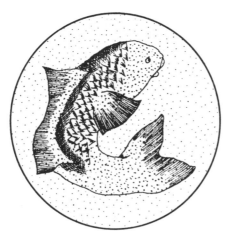

KAR-BEN COPIES, INC.   ROCKVILLE, MD

Published by Kar-Ben Copies, Inc., Rockville, MD
ISBN 0-930494-67-9

Text copyright © 1972 by Barbara Cohen
Illustrations copyright © by Joan Halpern

Reprinted by arrangement with Lothrop, Lee and Shepard Company
Printed in the United States of America
Library of Congress Catalog Card Number 87-80446
First Kar-Ben printing 1987

For Gene

When I was a little girl, I lived in an apartment house in New York City with Mama and Papa and my little brother Harry.

It was not very fancy, but Papa said we were lucky. We had our own bathroom. Mrs. Ginzburg, who lived downstairs, was also lucky—she had one too. Everyone else had to share the bathrooms in the hall.

Mama was a wonderful cook. It was well known that she made the finest chicken soup in Flatbush. Also very good tsimmis, noodle kugel, mondel bread, and stuffed cabbage.

But best of all was Mama's gefilte fish. Twice a year she made gefilte fish—in the fall for Rosh Hashanah, the Jewish New Year, and in the spring for Pesach, the festival of Passover. Aunt Malke and Uncle Moishe, cousin Zipporah, and Papa's friend Mr. Teitelbaum always came to our house for the Seder on the first night of Passover. They said that Mama's gefilte fish was not merely the best in Flatbush, nor the best in Brooklyn,

but actually the best gefilte fish in all of New York City.

Harry and I loved the Seder because we got to stay up until midnight. It took that long to say all the prayers, read the Passover story out of a book called the Haggadah, sing all the songs, and eat all the food. But I will tell you a secret. I was nine years old at the time I am telling you about, and I had never put a single piece of my mother's gefilte fish into my mouth.

Mama made her gefilte fish out of carp. For a day or two before Passover, carp was hard to find in the stores. All the ladies in the neighborhood had been buying it for their own gefilte fish. Mama liked to buy *her* carp at least a week before Passover to make sure she got the nicest, fattest, shiniest one. But Mama knew that a dead fish sitting in the icebox for a week would not be very good when the time came to make it into gefilte fish.

So Mama bought her fish live, and carried it home in a pail of water. All the way home it flopped and flipped because it was too big for the bucket. It would have died if Mama had left it in there.

As soon as she got home she would call, "Leah, run the water in the tub."

And I would put the rubber stopper in the drain and run some cold water into the bathtub. Then Mama would dump the carp out of the pail and into the tub.

The carp loved it there. He was always a big fish, but the tub was about four times as long as he was, and there was plenty of room for him to swim around.

Harry and I loved the carp. As long as he was there we didn't have to take baths.

Most of our friends took baths only once a week, but because we had our own tub, Mama made us bathe twice a week. "Otherwise," she said, "what is the use of having our own bathroom?" We didn't think it was fair, and we would gladly have moved into an apartment where tenants shared the bathrooms in the hall.

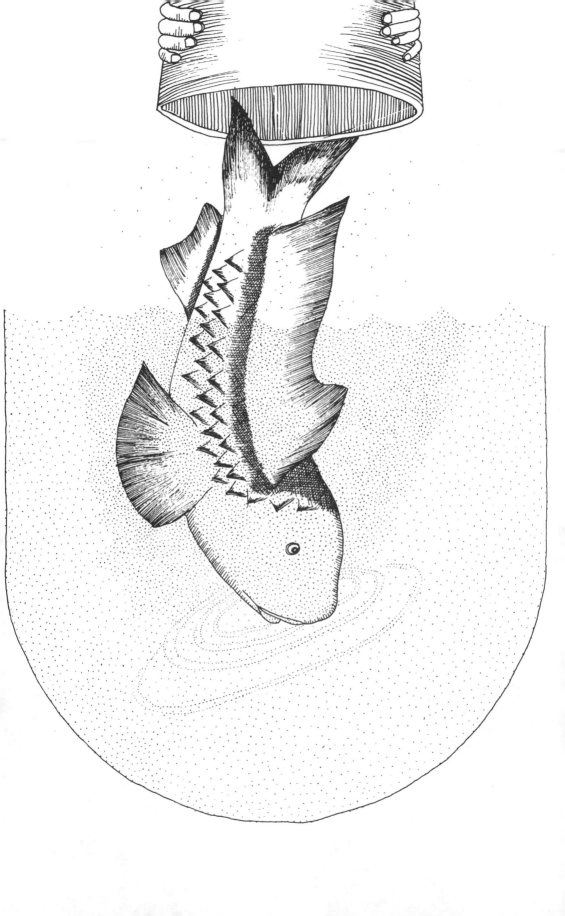

Except, of course, when we had a carp living in our bathtub. Every time Harry or I had to go to the toilet, we would grab a crust of bread or a rusty lettuce leaf from the kitchen. While we sat on the toilet, we fed the bread or the lettuce leaf to the carp. This made going to the bathroom really fun, instead of just a waste of time.

But the day always came when Mama marched into the bathroom carrying a big metal strainer and removed the stopper from the tub. The carp always seemed to know what was coming. He swam away from her as fast as he could, splashing the water all over her apron with his strong, flat tail. But he didn't have a chance. Before all the water was even out of the tub, Mama had caught him in her strainer. The way he was flopping around, he would have been on the floor before Mama got out of the bathroom door, so she dumped him right into her bucket and carried him to the kitchen.

We knew what she did with him when she got there, although we would never look. She killed him with a club! Then she scraped off the scales with a huge knife. The head, skin, and bones she boiled along with some carrots and onions in a big kettle of water to make stock. She put the flesh through a meat grinder with some more onions. After she had mixed it with matzo meal, eggs, and spices, she made it into balls. She took the stock and put it through the strainer to remove all the skin and bones, which she threw in the garbage.

She saved the stock for cooking the fish balls, which took hours. Harry and I would run out into the hall, but even there we couldn't escape the smell of fish.

Mama once told us that her Mama had not thrown away the skin. She had re-moved it so carefully from the carp that after the fish was cooked, she could put it back in the skin and bring it to the table. That's why the fish is called "gefilte," Mama said, which means "stuffed." At least, Harry and I were spared that!

You can see why we managed never to eat gefilte fish on Rosh Hashanah or Passover. Could *you* eat a friend?

The year I was nine was the worst of all. Most people think that all fish are pretty much the same, but this is definitely not true. Some carp are much more lovable than others, and that Passover we had an unusually playful and intelligent carp in our bathtub. He was larger than the others too. We were having extra company that year. Mrs. Ginzburg from downstairs and her unmarried daughter Elvira were coming up. Mr. Ginzburg had died six months before, and Mrs. Ginzburg just didn't have the heart to fuss and prepare for Passover.

This particular carp was also shinier than the others. His eyes were brighter and he seemed much livelier and friendlier. It got so that whenever Harry or I went into the bathroom, he'd swim right over to the end of the tub nearest the toilet as if he knew we were going to feed him. There was something about his mouth that made him seem to be smiling at us after he had eaten his bread crust or his lettuce.

In those days people like us, who lived in apartments in Flatbush, did not have pets. Harry and I would have loved owning a dog, a cat, or a bird, but Mama and Papa had never thought of such a thing, and it never occurred to us to ask. I'll tell you one thing, though. After that carp had been in our bathtub for nearly a week, we knew he was not just any old carp. He was our pet. In memory of Mr. Ginzburg, we called him Joe.

Two days before Passover, when I came home from school, Mama said, "You look after Harry, Leah. I have to go shopping, and I'll never get anything done if I have him trailing after me."

As soon as Mama was gone I looked at Harry, and Harry looked at me.

"We have to save Joe," I told him.

"We'll never have another chance," Harry agreed. "But what'll we do?"

"Mrs. Ginzburg has a bathtub," I reminded him.

Harry nodded. He saw what I meant right away.

I went to the kitchen, got the bucket, and carried it to the bathroom. Harry had already let all the water out of the tub. He helped lift Joe into the bucket. It was not easy for us because Joe must have weighed fifteen pounds, but we finally managed. We could add only a little water to the pail because it was already almost too heavy for us.

With both of us holding onto the handle and banging the bucket against every step, we lugged it downstairs to Mrs. Ginzburg's door. Then we rang her bell. She was very fat, and it took her a long time to waddle to the door, but she finally opened it.

"Why, Leah, Harry!" she said in surprise. "I'm very glad to see you. Won't you come in? Why are you carrying that bucket?" Mrs. Ginzburg was a very nice lady. She was always kind to us, even when she couldn't understand what we were doing.

We carried our bucket into Mrs. Ginzburg's front room. "May I ask what you have there?" she said politely.

"It's Joe," said Harry.

"Joe!" Mrs. Ginzburg closed her eyes and put her hand over her heart.

"We named him for Mr. Ginzburg," I explained quickly. "He smiles like Mr. Ginzburg."

"Oh . . ." Mrs. Ginzburg tried to smile too. Just then Joe twitched, his tail flashed over the top of the bucket, and a few drops of water dripped onto the oriental rug Mrs. Ginzburg had bought at Abraham and Straus with Mr. Ginzburg's Christmas bonus two years before. She glanced into the pail. "My goodness," she said, "he looks like a fish to me."

"He is a fish," I said. "He's the best fish in the world, and Mama can't kill him for Passover. She just can't. Please let him stay in your bathtub. Please. Just for a little while. Until I can figure out where to keep him for good."

"But Leah," Mrs. Ginzburg said, "I can't do that. Your Mama is my dear friend."

"If you don't let us put Joe in your bathtub soon," Harry pleaded, "he'll be dead. He's almost dead now."

Mrs. Ginzburg and I peered into the bucket. Harry was right. Joe didn't look too good. His scales weren't shiny bright any more, and he had stopped thrashing around. There was not enough water in the bucket for him.

"All right," said Mrs. Ginzburg. "But just for now." She ran some water into her tub, and we dumped our carp in. He no sooner felt all that clear cold water around him than he perked right up and started swimming. I took a few morsels of chopped meat I had stored away in my dress pocket and gave them to him. He smiled at me, just like always.

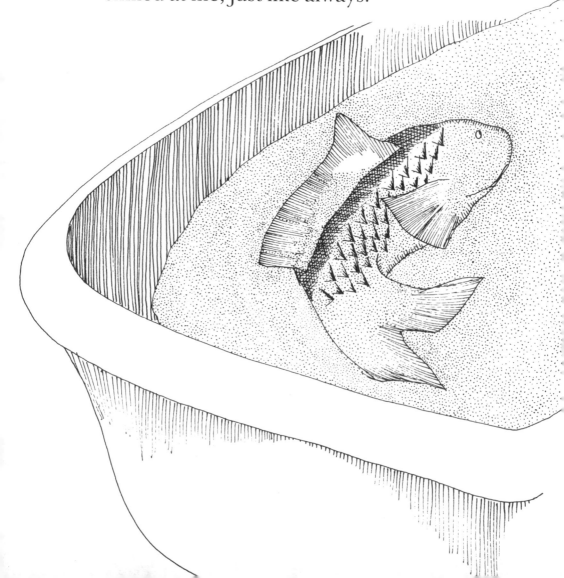

"This fish can't stay here," Mrs. Ginzburg warned. "I'm afraid I can't help hide him from your mother and father."

"What shall we do?" Harry asked me, blinking his eyes hard to keep back the tears.

"We'll go find Papa," I told him. "Papa doesn't cook, so maybe he'll understand. We'll have to find him before Mama gets home."

Papa was a cutter in a garment factory in Manhattan. He came home every night on the subway. Harry and I went down to the corner and waited by the stairs that led up from the station. After a while, we saw a big crowd of people who had just gotten off the train come up the stairs. Papa was with them. He was

I. R. T.
BKLYN. QUEENS
L. I. MAN.

holding onto the rail and climbing slowly, with his head down.

"Papa, Papa," we called.

He looked up and saw us. He straightened his shoulders, smiled, and ran quickly up the few remaining steps. "You came to meet me," he said. "That's very nice."

We started home together. I was holding one of Papa's hands, and Harry was holding the other. "Papa," I asked, "do you like gefilte fish?"

"Why, yes," he said, "of course I like gefilte fish. Your mother makes the best gefilte fish in all of Flatbush—in all of New York City. Everyone knows that."

"But would you like to eat gefilte fish," Harry asked, "if the fish was a friend of yours?"

Papa stood absolutely still right in the middle of the sidewalk. "Harry," he said, "Harry, what have you done to Mama's fish?"

"Leah did it too," Harry said.

Papa turned to me. Putting his hands on my shoulders, he looked right into my eyes. Papa's brown eyes were not large, but they were very bright. Most of the time his eyes smiled at us, but when he was angry or upset, like now, they could cut us like knives. "Leah," he said, "what did you do to Mama's fish?"

"Please, Papa," I said, "don't let Mama kill our fish. His name is Joe. We love him, and we want to keep him for a pet."

"Where is he now?" Papa asked.

I looked down at my hands and began to pick my fingernail. I didn't want to tell Papa where Joe was. But he put his hand on my chin and forced my face up. "Where's the fish now?" he asked again. His voice was gentle but those eyes were cutting me up.

"In Mrs. Ginzburg's bathtub," I mumbled.

Papa started walking again, faster now. We trailed along behind him, not holding his hands any more. He didn't say anything for a while. But when we got to our front stoop, he stopped to talk to us. "We are going to Mrs. Ginzburg's apartment and we are getting that fish," he said. "It's your mother's fish and it cost her a lot of money. She had to save a little out of what I give her each week just so she could buy such a big fish and make an extra nice Passover holiday for all of us." When we got to Mrs. Ginzburg's, Papa said to her, "We've come to take the fish home. I'm sorry for the trouble."

"Oh, he was no trouble," Mrs. Ginzburg said.

"Well, he would have been, as soon as you wanted to take a bath," Papa said.

We didn't say anything.

Mrs. Ginzburg let the water out of the tub. Papa didn't need a strainer to catch Joe. He just used his hands and the bucket.

It was much easier going back upstairs than it had been coming down. Papa carried the bucket. I ran the water, and without any ceremony Papa poured Joe in. He flitted through the water so gaily you'd think he was happy to be home. Foolish Joe.

"Carp are for eating," Papa said, "just like chicken. You always eat two helpings of chicken."

"We never met the chicken," I said.

Papa shook his head. "That's not the point, Leah. What God put on this earth to eat, we eat. We don't kill more creatures than we need, and we don't kill them for fun, but we eat what must be eaten. It would break Mama's heart if she realized you children didn't like to eat her gefilte fish. We won't tell her about any of this. Mrs. Ginzburg won't tell her either."

So nobody told Mama about how we had stolen her carp. Luckily, I was at school when she made Joe into gefilte fish. When I got home I asked Harry how he could have stood watching her catch Joe with her strainer and carry him off into the kitchen.

"I didn't watch," Harry said. "When I saw her go for that strainer and her club, I went right down to Mrs. Ginzburg's. But even there I could smell fish cooking."

Although Mama opened all the windows that afternoon, and no one else seemed to notice anything, Harry and I thought we smelled fish cooking for days.

We cried ourselves to sleep that night, and the next night too. Then we made ourselves stop crying. After that, we felt as if we were years older than Mama and Papa.

One night about a week after Passover, though, we were sitting in the kitchen helping Mama shell peas when Papa came home. As he walked through the door, we noticed that he was carrying something orange and black and white and furry in his arms. It was a beautiful big tri-color cat.

"They had too many cats hanging around the loft," Papa said. "This one seemed so friendly and pretty that I brought her home."

Mama seemed surprised, but she let the cat stay. She was a clean cat, and good at chasing the rats out of our kitchen. We called her Joe. Mama couldn't understand that.

I'm an old lady now—a grandmother, as a matter of fact. My daughters buy gefilte fish in jars at the supermarket. They think their Uncle Harry and I don't eat it because it isn't as good as the kind our mother made. We don't tell them that we never ate Mama's either.